Extreme Cars

HYPERCARS

Steve Rendle

PowerKiDS press

New York

Published in 2022 by The Rosen Publishing Group, Inc.
29 East 21st Street, New York, NY 10010

Originally Published in English by Haynes Publishing under the title: *Extreme Cars Pocket Manual* © Haynes Publishing 2019

Cataloging-in-Publication Data

Names: Rendle, Steve.
Title: Hypercars / Steve Rendle.
Description: New York : PowerKids Press, 2022. | Series: Extreme cars | Includes glossary and index.
Identifiers: ISBN 9781725332379 (pbk.) | ISBN 9781725332393 (library bound) | ISBN 9781725332386 (6 pack) | ISBN 9781725332409 (ebook)
Subjects: LCSH: Sports cars--Juvenile literature.
Classification: LCC TL236.R448 2022 | DDC 629.228--dc23

Design by Richard Parsons and James Robertson

The following agencies have given permission to use their images:

Photographs supplied by the individual car manufacturers.
Additional images published with the permission of Getty.
Cover, huang zixing/Shutterstock.com; Cover, p. 1 Double Brain/Shutterstock.com; pp. 3-5, 8, 9, 12, 13, 16, 17, 20, 21, 24, 25, 28-32 Carlos Caetano/Shutterstock.com.

Manufactured in the United States of America

CPSIA Compliance Information: Batch #CWPK22. For Further Information contact Rosen Publishing, New York, New York at 1-800-237-9932.

CONTENTS

INTRODUCTION

This book is about hypercars, and we've picked some of the most extreme ones in the world. You might wonder what made us select some but not others. Well, for a start, all the cars in this book have been, or will be, available to buy, as long as buyers have enough money and, in some cases, if they meet the conditions that the car manufacturer sets. You won't see these cars every day—and there are some that you will probably never see—but they are all out there on the world's roads or tracks somewhere!

Most of the cars are very modern and fitted with the latest technology. There are a few older cars too. However old they are, though, all the cars included have been selected because they are built to provide an incredible experience for the driver—but not necessarily for passengers. In most cases, the cars need a skilled driver to make the most of them. Some are racing cars for the road, while others are road cars that were built so that they could also be raced.

Every one of the cars included has extreme performance—either top speed or acceleration—and most are able to corner like racing cars. Of course, they all sound incredible. Some have road-car luxuries too, such as leather trim, in-car entertainment, air conditioning, and satnav.

Perhaps one day you might be lucky enough to get behind the wheel of one of the ultimate machines featured in the following pages and find out just how exciting they can be. Until then, enjoy reading and daydreaming about them!

ABBREVIATIONS AND THEIR MEANINGS

bhp	brake horsepower—available power of an engine
cc	cubic centimeters—volume of engine cylinders added together
in	inches—used for wheel sizes
kg	kilograms—unit of weight
kph	kilometers per hour—unit of speed
kW	kilowatts—unit of power
lb	pounds— unit of weight
lb ft	pound foot—unit of torque
LCD	liquid-crystal display
mm	millimeters—unit of length
mph	miles per hour—unit of speed
Nm	newton meter—unit of torque
rpm	revolutions per minute—the number of turns in one minute
s	seconds—unit of time
V6	V-shaped engine with six cylinders (three on each side of the "V")
V8	V-shaped engine with eight cylinders (four on each side of the "V")
V12	V-shaped engine with 12 cylinders (six on each side of the "V")
W16	W-shaped engine with 16 cylinders (four on each arm of the "W")

ALL ABOUT TIRES

Tires have codes that explain their sizes, and these codes are usually printed on the edge of each tire. As an example, a tire might have a code like **205/50 R15**.

205	means that the tire is 205 mm wide.
50	means that the "profile" (thickness, or height) of the tire is 50 percent of its width. The smaller the number, the thinner the tire.
R	means that the tire is a "radial"-type tire—it is made from layers of material that run in layers at right angles to the direction in which the tire rolls.
15	means that the tire is designed to fit on a 15-in-diameter wheel.

ASTON MARTIN ONE-77

Aston Martin's first "hypercar," inspired by James Bond

- The 77 cars were built between 2009 and 2012.
- The car's design team was inspired by high-tech DTM racing cars.
- Buyers had to pay a deposit of over $200,000 when they placed their order.
- The cars have a carbon-fiber monocoque and hand-shaped aluminium body.

Aston Martins are already pretty special, and most people think of them as supercars, so how do you make them better? In 2008, Aston Martin decided to build a "hypercar" as a new flagship for its range, with a 7.2-liter, 750-bhp (559 kW) V12 engine, and a top speed of 220 mph (354 kph). The result was the incredible One-77, which cost about $1.9 million then and costs even more today!

This was Aston Martin's answer to the equally extreme Bugatti Veyron and Ferrari Enzo. The car's name, One-77, was probably chosen as a reference to the most famous Aston Martin driver, fictional British Secret Service agent James Bond (also known as 007). It also indicated that only 77 cars would be built. In case the One-77 wasn't exclusive enough, seven were produced as special Q-Series cars, which allowed the wealthy owners to order their cars with special custom paint schemes and interior trim. Q-Series was a reference to another character in the James Bond stories—known as "Q"—who provided Bond's amazing spy gadgets.

STATISTICS ASTON MARTIN ONE-77

Price (new)	$1.9 million
Max speed	Over 220 mph (354 kph)
0–62 mph (0–100 kph)	Under 3.7 s
Engine type	Alloy, quad-cam, 48-valve, normally aspirated V12
Engine capacity	7,312 cc
Max power	750 bhp (559 kW)
Max torque	750 Nm (553 lb ft)
Transmission	Rear-mounted 6-speed automated manual gearbox, carbon-fiber propeller shaft, limited-slip differential
Suspension	Front and rear double wishbones, front and rear anti-roll bars, pushrod-actuated coil springs, and adjustable monotube dampers. Electrically adjustable for ride height and rate change
Wheels and tires	20-in forged alloy front and rear wheels; 255/35 ZR20 front tires; 335/30 ZR20 rear tires
Curb weight	3,594 lb (1,630 kg)
Length	181.1 in (4,600 mm)
Width	86.8 in (2,205 mm), with mirrors
Height	48.1 in (1,222 mm)
Year introduced	2009

AN AUTOMATIC REAR SPOILER IS RAISED AT HIGH SPEEDS.

KOENIGSEGG JESKO

The best so far from a company that builds only hypercars

- Jeskos are available in high-downforce (track) and low-drag (road) versions.
- A G-force meter can be fitted on the dashboard as an option.
- The "Smartwheel" steering wheel has two small touchscreens built in.
- Koenigsegg's factory codename for the car was "Ragnorok"!

The Jesko has a specially designed twin-turbo 5.0-liter, 1,600-bhp (1,193 kW) V8 engine and high-tech computer systems, and is designed to excel on the track. Although it has high-downforce aerodynamics and race-inspired suspension, it has plenty of creature comforts for the driver!

Specialist Swedish hypercar builder Koenigsegg unveiled the stunning Jesko at the Geneva Motor Show in March 2019. The car has been developed from the Koenigsegg Agera and is named after the father of company founder Christian von Koenigsegg. Advanced electronic systems include a "SmartCenter" instrument display (which has a copy of the car's owners' manual installed) that rotates with the steering wheel. The display's center section turns to keep the vital gauges level for easy reading. A "UPOD" (Ultimate Power On Demand) system automatically selects the best gear for maximum acceleration. The system can jump gears without needing to change gear in sequence. The first production cars became available in 2020, but all 125 sold out quickly.

STATISTICS KOENIGSEGG JESKO

Price (new)	$3 million
Max speed	277 mph (456 kph)
0–60 mph (0–97 kph)	2.5 s
Engine type	Twin-turbo V8
Engine capacity	5.0 liters
Max power	1,600 bhp (1,193 kW) on E85 biofuel; 1,280 bhp (209 kW) on standard fuel
Max torque	1,500 Nm (1,106 lb ft) at 5,100 rpm
Transmission	9-speed Koenigsegg Light Speed Transmission (LST)
Suspension	Wishbones with electronically controlled "Triplex" three-damper system front and rear
Wheels and tires	20-in front wheels; 21-in rear wheels; 265/35 R20 front tires; 345/30 R21 rear tires
Curb weight	3,131 lb (1,420 kg)
Length	181.5 in (4,610 mm)
Width	79.9 in (2,029 mm)
Height	47.6 in (1,209 mm)
Year introduced	2020

THE FACTORY IN SWEDEN CAN ADJUST THE SUSPENSION DAMPERS ONLINE!

McLAREN P1

Stunning looks and a superhero performance to match

- Only 375 standard P1s were built, along with just over 40 GTRs and five LMs.
- F1 Champion Jenson Button sold his P1 with only 551 miles (887 km) on the dash.
- The P1 can travel 12 miles (19 km) at 30 mph (48 kph) using just the electric motor.
- The P1 comes with air conditioning, satnav, and audio system, but mats cost extra!

The McLaren P1 followed in the footsteps of the incredible McLaren F1, and its stunning styling maximizes aerodynamic performance. Describing the car's shape, its designer Frank Stephenson said: "It's as though we stuck a tube inside and sucked all the air out." This extreme car was tested in extreme conditions, in the cold of the Arctic Circle and the heat of Death Valley!

The car has a Drag Reduction System (DRS), as used on F1 cars, that reduces the car's aerodynamic drag when a button on the steering wheel is pressed to move the rear wing flat. The Instant Power Assist System (IPAS) is an electric motor that works automatically to boost engine power or can be operated by a button on the steering wheel. In 2015, McLaren introduced the P1 GTR – a track-only version with power increased to 986 bhp (735 kW) and built-in air jacks! The ultra-rare road-legal P1 LM uses the same 986-bhp engine as the GTR, but has special lightweight components, improved aerodynamics, and no air jacks.

STATISTICS MCLAREN P1

Price (new)	$1.2 million
Max speed	217 mph (350 kph)
0–62 mph (0–100 kph)	2.8 s
Engine type	Twin-turbo V8 internal combustion engine, plus IPAS electric motor
Engine capacity	3,799 cc
Max power	727 bhp (542 kW) for V8 engine, plus 176 bhp (131 kW) from IPAS electric motor, giving a total of 903 bhp (673 kW)
Max torque	720 Nm (531 lb ft) from internal combustion engine, plus 260 Nm (192 lb ft) from IPAS electric motor, giving a total of 980 Nm (723 lb ft)
Transmission	7-speed dual-clutch gearbox
Suspension	Double wishbones front and rear with Race Active Chassis Control (RCC)
Wheels and tires	19-in front wheels; 20-in rear wheels; 245/35 R19 front tires; 315/30 R20 rear tires
Curb weight	3,410 lb (1,547 kg)
Length	180.6 in (4,588 mm)
Width	76.6 in (1,946 mm)
Height	46.8 in (1,188 mm)
Year introduced	2013

THE P1 GTR WAS OFFERED ONLY TO OWNERS WHO HAD ALREADY BOUGHT A P1.

PAGANI HUAYRA BC

Specially developed materials for one of the lightest-ever hypercars

- The Huayra is named after Huarya-tata, an Andean wind god.
- One customer ordered a Huarya BC with a factory-fitted cupholder!
- Racing-car manufacturer Dallara helped optimize the car's aerodynamics.
- When it first appeared, the Huarya BC was the lightest hypercar available.

Horacio Pagani has been a world leader in hypercar design since his first production car—the stunning Zonda C12—appeared in 1999. The original Huayra coupe appeared in 2011. The Huayra BC has the same roof panel as the coupe, but almost every other component has been redesigned to save weight. Anything that could be made lighter has been!

The "BC" in the car's name stands for Benny Caiola, who was the very first customer to buy a Pagani car. The car was designed to be road-legal but also super-quick for track days. Each car comes with two sets of wheels and tires—one for the road and one for the track. The car uses specially developed lightweight materials, including a "Carbo-Titanium" chassis and "CrMoVanadio" metal for the front and rear suspension frames. The car's high-tech systems include active aerodynamics, with flaps that move automatically to stabilize the car and maximize downforce for cornering, and carbon-ceramic brakes. Only 20 Huarya BCs have been built.

STATISTICS PAGANI HUAYRA BC

Price (new)	$2.5 million
Max speed	230 mph (370 kph)
0–62 mph (0–100 kph)	2.8 s
Engine type	Mercedes-Benz AMG, twin-turbo V12
Engine capacity	5,980 cc
Max power	740 bhp (552 kW) at 6,200 rpm
Max torque	1,000 Nm (738 lb ft) at 4,000 rpm
Transmission	7-speed automated manual transmission with electronic mechanical differential
Suspension	Double wishbones front and rear with front and rear anti-roll bars, coil springs, and adjustable dampers
Wheels and tires	20-in front wheels; 21-in rear wheels; 255/30 R20 front tires; 355/25 R21 rear tires
Curb weight	2,685 lb (1,218 kg)
Length	181.3 in (4,605 mm)
Width	80.2 in (2,036 mm)
Height	46 in (1,169 mm)
Year introduced	2016

THE CAR HAS AN ELECTRIC PARKING BRAKE TO SAVE WEIGHT.

PORSCHE 918 SPYDER

One of the world's fastest-accelerating production cars

- The "Weissach" package, which used lightweight parts, cost $84,000 extra!
- The 918 Spyder is available in left-hand drive only.
- An optional "fast charger" charges the hybrid-system battery in 25 minutes.
- In a road test, *Car and Driver* magazine clocked 0–60 mph (0–97 kph) in 2.2 seconds.

The Porsche 918 Spyder is a stunning hybrid hypercar powered by a 600-bhp (447 kW) V8, along with two electric motors. One electric motor drives the front wheels, and the other is coupled with the V8 engine to drive the rear wheels.

The 918 Spyder first appeared as a concept car in 2010, and after more than 2,000 possible customers showed interest, Porsche decided to put the car into production. Exactly 918 cars were built, and the last one rolled off the production line in June 2015. Optional metallic paint cost an extra $63,000!

A one-off 918 RSR "racing laboratory" was also built, with a coupe body. The RSR was aimed at racing but is not actually eligible for any racing series! The RSR still has two electric motors, but each motor drives one of the front wheels, while the V8 engine drives the rear wheels. The electric motors don't run all the time, but can provide a 200-bhp (150 kW) power boost for around 8 seconds.

STATISTICS PORSCHE 918 SPYDER

Price (new)	$845,000
Max speed	218 mph (351 kph)
0–62 mph (0–100 kph)	2.4 s
Engine type	Normally aspirated V8, plus two electric motors
Engine capacity	4,593 cc
Max power	608 bhp (447 kW) maximum from V8 engine, plus 286 bhp (210 kW) maximum from electric motors, and a combined maximum available total of 887 bhp (652 kW) at 8,500 rpm
Max torque	1,280 Nm (944 lb ft)
Transmission	7-speed PDK gearbox, four-wheel-drive
Suspension	Wishbones and links, with Porsche Active Suspension Management (PASM) adaptive dampers
Wheels and tires	20-in front wheels; 21-in rear wheels; 265/35 R20 front tires; 325/30 R21 rear tires
Curb weight	3,602 lb (1,634 kg)
Length	182.8 in (4,643 mm)
Width	76.4 in (1,940 mm)
Height	45.9 in (1,167 mm)
Year introduced	2013

THE CAR'S DETACHABLE ROOF PANEL CAN BE STORED UNDER THE HOOD.

SSC TUATARA

A stunning American-built hypercar inspired by jet fighter planes

- The car has so far taken 10 years to develop, and 100 cars will be built.
- The Tuatara is named after a lizard-like reptile from New Zealand.
- The car has a digital dash display called a Human-Machine Interface (HMI).
- The 5.9-liter twin-turbo V8 engine was built specially for the Tuatura.

SSC (Shelby Super Cars) is an American company that produced the SSC Ultimate Aero in 2007, which was briefly the world's fastest production car, beating the Bugatti Veyron's record. The SSC Tuatara is the follow-up to the Ultimate Aero and is designed to beat a maximum speed of 300 mph (483 kph). Though it hasn't reached that speed yet, it set a record in 2021, traveling 282.9 mph (455.3 kph).

The car has extremely good aerodynamics, with a computer-controlled active rear wing that automatically adjusts to give maximum downforce and acts as an airbrake when the car is braking. The twin-turbo V8 is tuned to produce 1,750 bhp (1,305 kW)! Three suspension modes are provided: "Sport" for road driving, "Track" for maximum performance, and "Front Lift," which raises the suspension for speed bumps! The car's equipment includes digital driver display, touch-screen control system, side cameras for blind-spot vision, and a premium in-car entertainment system. The first customer car Tuatara was unveiled in 2020.

STATISTICS SSC TUATARA

Price (new)	$1.6 million
Max speed	282.9 mph (455.3 kph)
0–60 mph (0–97 kph)	2.5 s
Engine type	Twin-turbo V8
Engine capacity	5.9 liters
Max power	1,750 bhp (1,305 kW) on E85 biofuel; 1,350 bhp (1,007 kW) on 91-octane fuel
Max torque	1,735 Nm (1,280 lb ft)
Transmission	7-speed semi-automatic gearbox
Suspension	height adjustable with remote damper reservoirs and coil-over springs
Wheels and tires	20-in front and rear wheels; 245/35 R20 front tires; 345/30 R20 rear tires
Curb weight	2,749 lb (1,247 kg)
Length	182.4 in (4,633 mm)
Width	81.3 in (2,065 mm)
Height	42.0 in (1,067 mm)
Year introduced	2019

THE CAR'S "BUBBLE-CANOPY" COCKPIT WAS INSPIRED BY JET FIGHTER DESIGN.

GLOSSARY

air jack: a mechanism used for lifting a vehicle off the ground by means of an inflatable support (to change a tire, for example)

chassis: steel tubes that carry the engine, seats, and other parts of a car

coupe: a two-door car often seating only two people

dampers: devices in a suspension system that prevent bouncing up and down

hypercars: the most superior and high-performance cars on the worldwide market

monocoque: a type of vehicle structure in which the body is combined with the chassis as a single unit

normally aspirated: describing an internal combustion engine in which air intake depends only on atmospheric pressure

satnav: a satellite-based navigation system

suspension: a system of springs and other devices on a car that reduces the shaking and bumping caused by uneven surfaces

torque: a rotating force produced by an engine's crankshaft

transmission: the gear that transmits power from a car or truck's engine to the wheels

wishbone: an automobile suspension that resembles the wishbone of a bird

FOR MORE INFO

BOOKS

Adamson, Thomas K. *Porsche 918 Spyder.* Mendota Heights, MN: North Star Editions, 2019.

Smith, Ryan. *Aston Martin.* New York, NY: AV2, 2021.

Venturi, Luca, et al. *Pagani Hypercars.* New York, NY: Rizzoli, 2018.

WEBSITES

Aston Martin Heritage
www.astonmartin.com/en-us/our-world/heritage
Discover the history of this famous car.

Koenigsegg Automotive AB
www.koenigsegg.com/
Check out the stunning cars made by this company.

Supercar vs. Hypercar
www.continentalautosports.com/ferrari-information/supercar-vs-hypercar/
Learn the difference between these top-performing vehicles.

Publisher's note to parents and teachers: Our editors have reviewed the websites listed here to make sure they're suitable for students. However, websites may change frequently. Please note that students should always be supervised when they access the internet.

INDEX